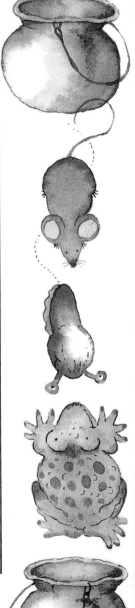

WOBBLY WITCH

and

A DOG NAMED BRIAN

ILLUSTRATED BY DIANA CATCHPOLE

P

PARRAGON

For Claire - C.S.

This is a Parragon Book

©Parragon 1997

Parragon
13-17 Avonbridge Trading Estate
Atlantic Road, Avonmouth
Bristol. BS11 9QD

Produced by The Templar Company plc,
Pippbrook Mill, London Road, Dorking,
Surrey RH4 1JE

Designed by Janie Louise Hunt
Edited by Caroline Steeden
Printed and bound in Italy
ISBN 0 75252 504 2

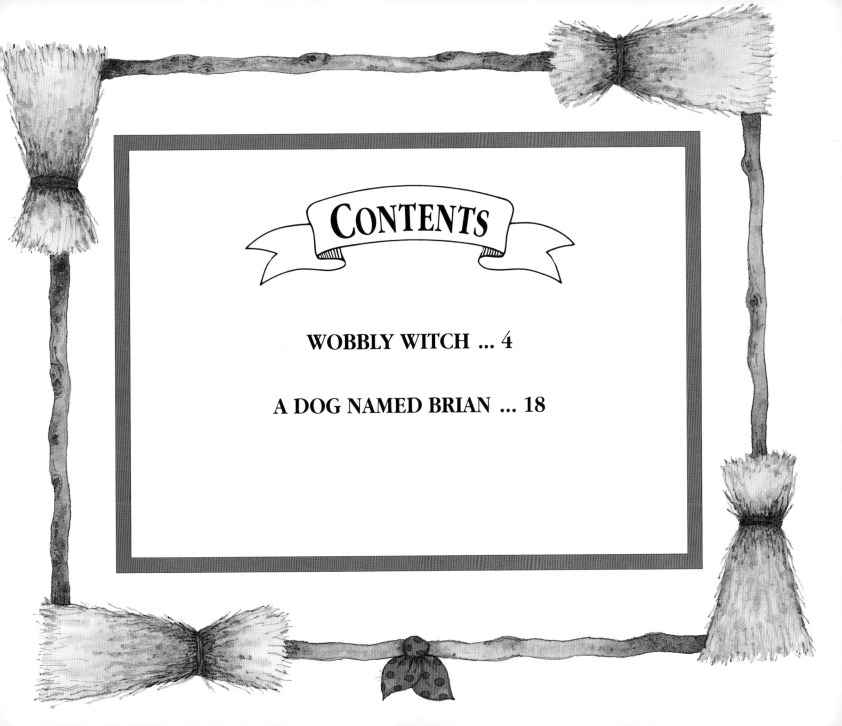

CONTENTS

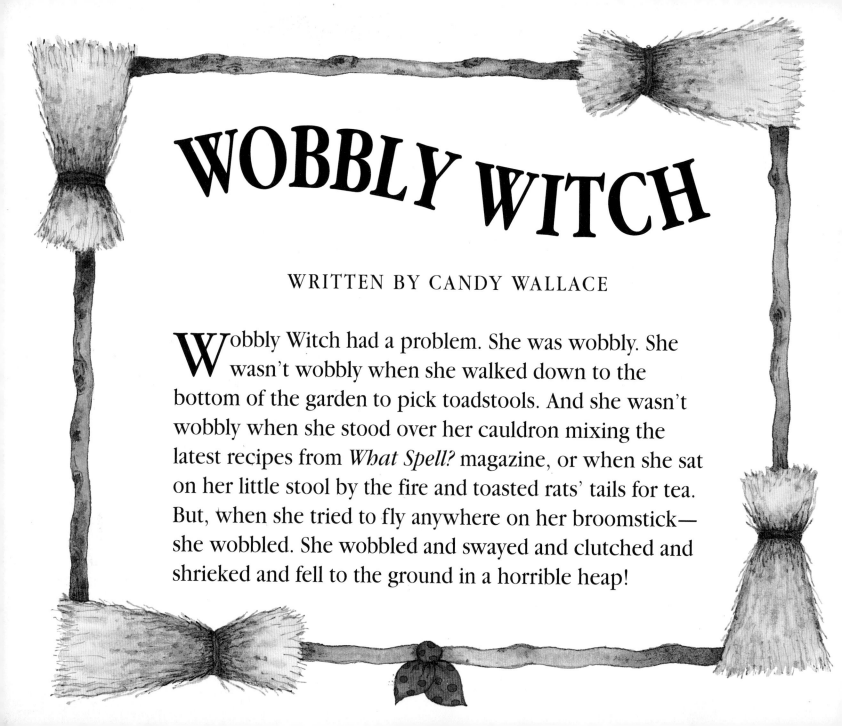

WOBBLY WITCH

WRITTEN BY CANDY WALLACE

Wobbly Witch had a problem. She was wobbly. She wasn't wobbly when she walked down to the bottom of the garden to pick toadstools. And she wasn't wobbly when she stood over her cauldron mixing the latest recipes from *What Spell?* magazine, or when she sat on her little stool by the fire and toasted rats' tails for tea. But, when she tried to fly anywhere on her broomstick— she wobbled. She wobbled and swayed and clutched and shrieked and fell to the ground in a horrible heap!

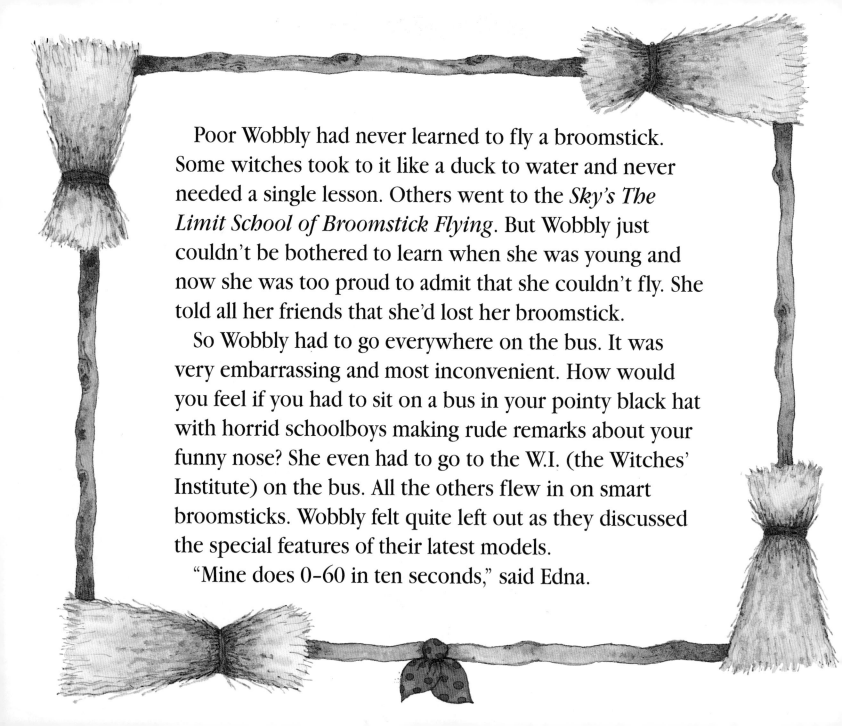

Poor Wobbly had never learned to fly a broomstick. Some witches took to it like a duck to water and never needed a single lesson. Others went to the *Sky's The Limit School of Broomstick Flying*. But Wobbly just couldn't be bothered to learn when she was young and now she was too proud to admit that she couldn't fly. She told all her friends that she'd lost her broomstick.

So Wobbly had to go everywhere on the bus. It was very embarrassing and most inconvenient. How would you feel if you had to sit on a bus in your pointy black hat with horrid schoolboys making rude remarks about your funny nose? She even had to go to the W.I. (the Witches' Institute) on the bus. All the others flew in on smart broomsticks. Wobbly felt quite left out as they discussed the special features of their latest models.

"Mine does 0-60 in ten seconds," said Edna.

Wobbly might never have learned to fly, if it hadn't been for the birthday present and her cat, Boris.

On Wobbly's birthday the postman brought lots of lovely birthday cards, a couple of small parcels and one big one that was very long and very thin. One parcel had a smart new witch's hat in it, from Wobbly's friend Vera.

The other one was a silver balloon on a string. It had "Happy Birthday!" on it and floated up into the air when she opened the parcel. Wobbly was very pleased.

"Now what can this long one be, Boris?" said Wobbly to her cat, who, like all cats was very curious. Boris snuggled up to Wobbly and purred. He'd had a large kipper for breakfast and was in a very good mood.

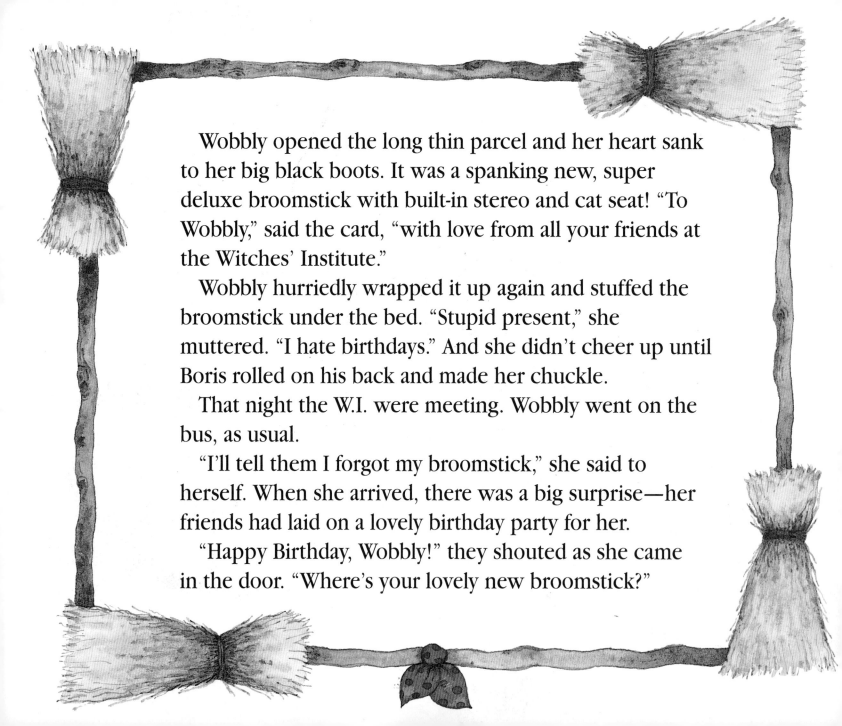

Wobbly opened the long thin parcel and her heart sank to her big black boots. It was a spanking new, super deluxe broomstick with built-in stereo and cat seat! "To Wobbly," said the card, "with love from all your friends at the Witches' Institute."

Wobbly hurriedly wrapped it up again and stuffed the broomstick under the bed. "Stupid present," she muttered. "I hate birthdays." And she didn't cheer up until Boris rolled on his back and made her chuckle.

That night the W.I. were meeting. Wobbly went on the bus, as usual.

"I'll tell them I forgot my broomstick," she said to herself. When she arrived, there was a big surprise—her friends had laid on a lovely birthday party for her.

"Happy Birthday, Wobbly!" they shouted as she came in the door. "Where's your lovely new broomstick?"

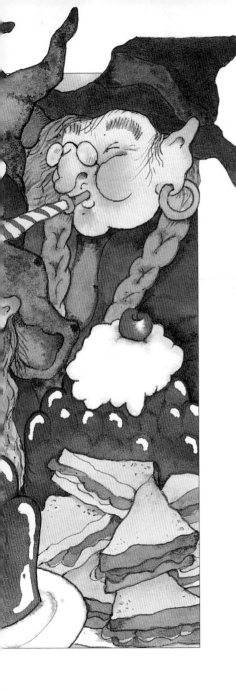

Wobbly soon forgot to feel miserable. There was a huge birthday cake decorated with little bats made out of icing. There were extra wobbly jellies in her honour and lots of delicious sandwiches. It all went well, until somebody mentioned playing games.

They played Hide and Shriek, Pass the Toad and Pin the Tail on the Rat. But the next game was Broomstick Races. Soon, all the witches but Wobbly were whizzing up and down on their broomsticks, cackling and having fun. Wobbly looked on and sulked.

"Right, that's it!" she said. "I'm going home. I hate parties!" And she sneaked out.

When she arrived home, she expected Boris to meet her at the door. But there was no sign of him.

"Great lazy lump," thought Wobbly, crossly. "He's still sleeping off that kipper I gave him!" But when she looked on his favourite chair, he wasn't there. "Boris, Boris, where are you?" she called. But there was no answering miaow.

Feeling worried, Wobbly went outside and called his name again. It was a dark night with a bright, shiny moon and she strained her eyes to see. Then something caught her eye. Right at the top of a tree, she saw a flash of light. It was her birthday balloon, caught on a branch. Suddenly, the branch shook.

"Miaeeeeeew!" It was Boris! He had chased the balloon to the top of the tallest tree in the garden and now he was stuck!

"Oh, you silly cat!" shrieked Wobbly. "How am I going to get you down from there!"

"Miaeeeeeew!" wailed poor Boris.

Wobbly rushed to fetch an old ladder. But when she put it against the tree it didn't even reach half way up. Poor Boris seemed to be clinging on by a claw. His miaows grew fainter…

Wobbly stamped her foot and turned and rushed into her cottage. She dashed up the stairs and into the bedroom.

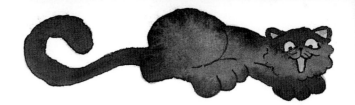

On her hands and knees, she grabbed the parcel under the bed and hurried downstairs with it, tearing off the paper as she went.

"Don't worry, Boris!" she cried. "I'll rescue you!" Leaping astride the gleaming new broomstick, she closed her eyes and took a deep breath…

Up she went, up into the sky without a single wobble! As she climbed higher and higher, her old hat blew off and was carried away by the wind. The broomstick swept round in a curve and came to a stop, hovering over the branch where poor Boris was clinging on for dear life.

Wobbly grabbed him and put him on the broomstick behind her. Then she untangled the balloon, tied it to the broomstick and swept down to a smooth landing outside her front door. Boris walked off the broomstick as if nothing had happened.

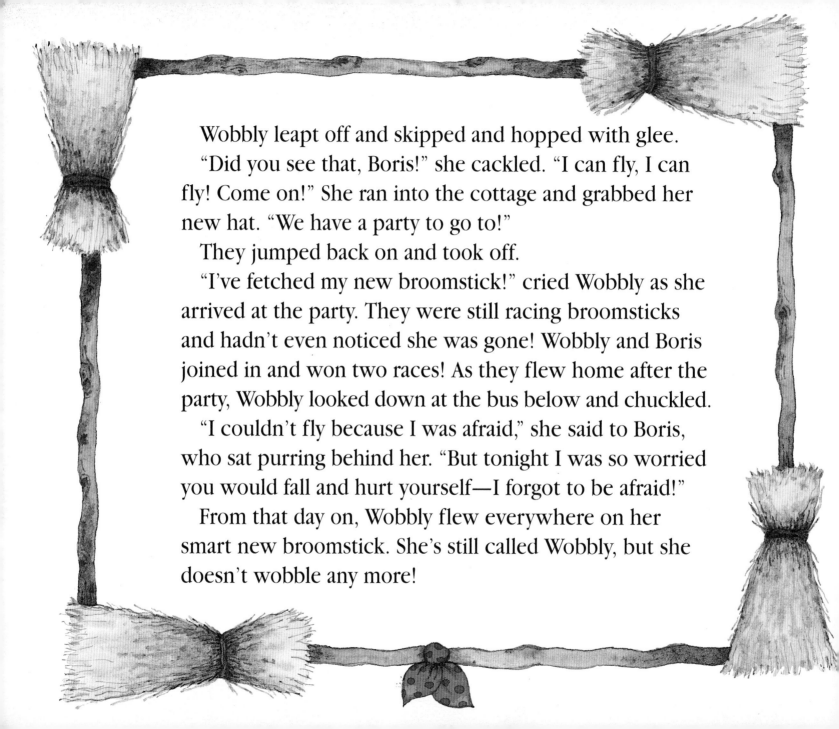

Wobbly leapt off and skipped and hopped with glee.

"Did you see that, Boris!" she cackled. "I can fly, I can fly! Come on!" She ran into the cottage and grabbed her new hat. "We have a party to go to!"

They jumped back on and took off.

"I've fetched my new broomstick!" cried Wobbly as she arrived at the party. They were still racing broomsticks and hadn't even noticed she was gone! Wobbly and Boris joined in and won two races! As they flew home after the party, Wobbly looked down at the bus below and chuckled.

"I couldn't fly because I was afraid," she said to Boris, who sat purring behind her. "But tonight I was so worried you would fall and hurt yourself—I forgot to be afraid!"

From that day on, Wobbly flew everywhere on her smart new broomstick. She's still called Wobbly, but she doesn't wobble any more!

A DOG NAMED BRIAN

WRITTEN BY CANDY WALLACE

Wimple the Witch was having trouble with her cat. Now, as you know, all witches need a cat. No cat, no spells. They just won't work without the magic spark from a cat's eyes. So when Wimple had trouble with her cat — it was big trouble.

"You're a great big useless heap of fur," she shrieked at Montgomery, who was lying on his back with his paws in the air, snoring. "Can't you think of anything better to do than sleep all day?"

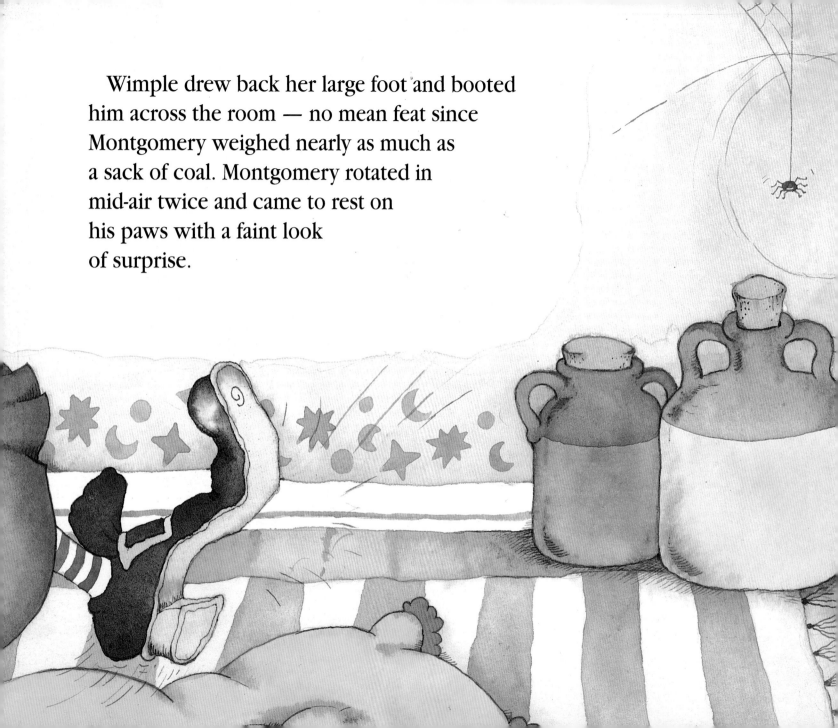

Wimple drew back her large foot and booted
him across the room — no mean feat since
Montgomery weighed nearly as much as
a sack of coal. Montgomery rotated in
mid-air twice and came to rest on
his paws with a faint look
of surprise.

His feelings were more hurt than anything. True, he had slowed down a trifle lately, but frankly, he was getting on a bit now. He'd used up eight-and-a-half lives and all he wanted was a bit of peace.

Wimple put her hands on her hips and glowered at Montgomery, who had keeled over on the spot and fallen into an instant slumber.

"Right!" she screamed. "That's it!" It was time to get another cat. One she could rely on. In two shakes of a rat's tail she was astride her broomstick and on her way to the *Paws for Thought* cat agency.

"I want a sleek, hardworking black cat with a flash of genius. Experience in turning princes into frogs and vice versa would be preferred," she said, to the bored-looking witch behind the counter.

"No," the assistant said.

"What do you mean — no?" said Wimple.

"No cats left on our books. We've had a run on them this week."

Wimple turned purple.

"All we've got left is a dog called Brian." While Wimple stood there, speechless, the assistant went into a back room and came back with a huge bloodhound who looked rather depressed. He knew just what would happen. They always took one look at him and shrieked with laughter.

He'd spent three years learning to be a Witch's Personal Assistant and now nobody would hire him.

"I'll take him!" said Wimple suddenly. She was a desperate witch. "I just wish he wasn't quite so big."

The first problem was that there was no way Brian was going to ride on the broomstick. When he got on it it just

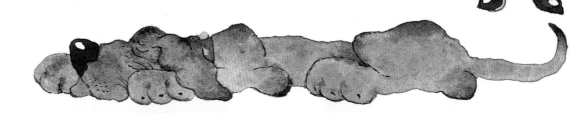

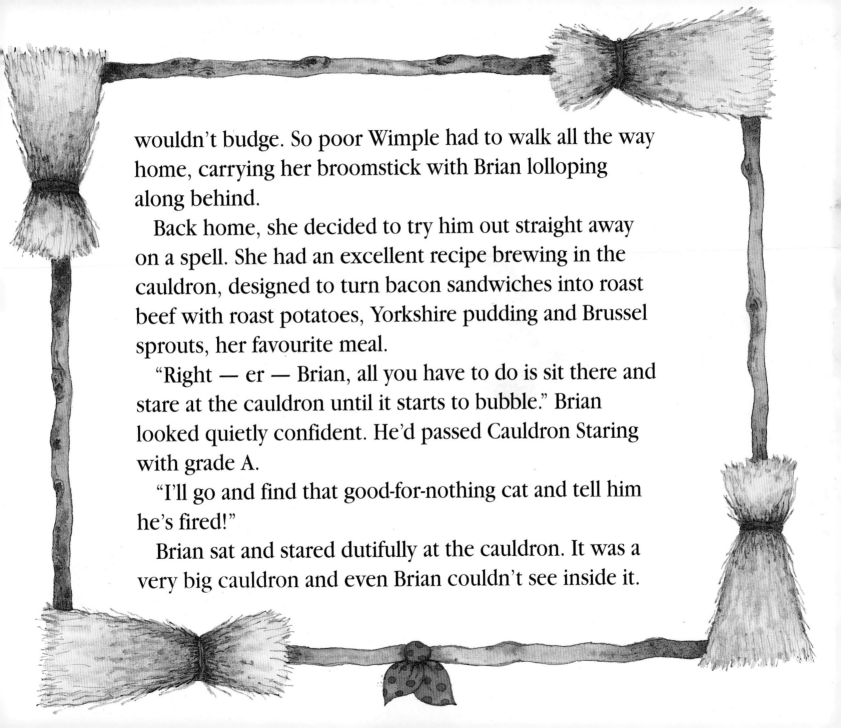

wouldn't budge. So poor Wimple had to walk all the way home, carrying her broomstick with Brian lolloping along behind.

Back home, she decided to try him out straight away on a spell. She had an excellent recipe brewing in the cauldron, designed to turn bacon sandwiches into roast beef with roast potatoes, Yorkshire pudding and Brussel sprouts, her favourite meal.

"Right — er — Brian, all you have to do is sit there and stare at the cauldron until it starts to bubble." Brian looked quietly confident. He'd passed Cauldron Staring with grade A.

"I'll go and find that good-for-nothing cat and tell him he's fired!"

Brian sat and stared dutifully at the cauldron. It was a very big cauldron and even Brian couldn't see inside it.

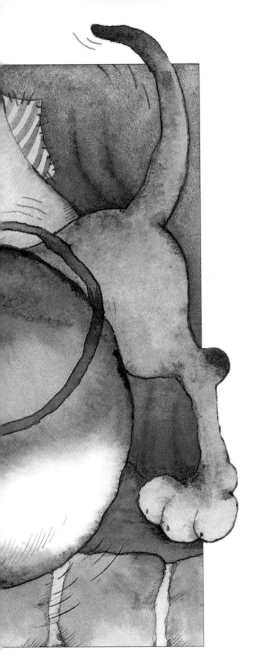

So he didn't know whether it was bubbling or not. He thought he'd better check and put his paws up on the top of the cauldron to look in. The big pot swayed and tilted and crash! It toppled over. All the bubbling liquid flowed onto the floor — and over Montgomery who was busy escaping from Wimple. Montgomery felt very strange for a minute and then turned into a Brussel sprout. Wimple, following behind, stopped dead in her tracks.

"You stupid dog! Quick, we'll have to mix another spell. She thumbed through her recipe book until she found Brussel Sprout — Into Cat, page 62. "We need some toadstools. Go and get some this minute!" Poor Brian was feeling very embarrassed and loped off into the garden, determined he would prove himself this time.
He came back carrying a basket full of toadstools.

Strangely enough, Wimple didn't seem pleased. She was staring out of the window with eyes like saucers, clenching her fists.

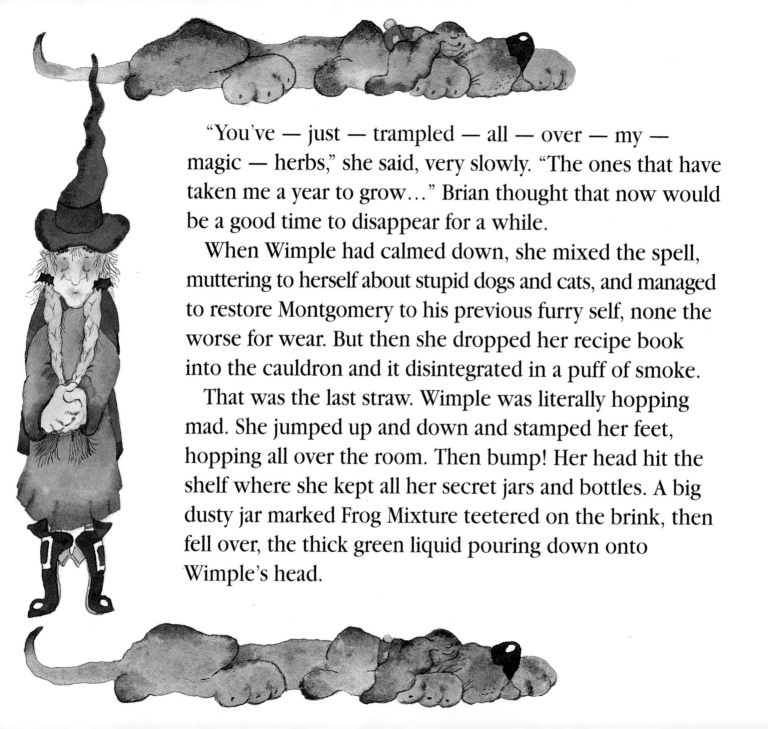

"You've — just — trampled — all — over — my — magic — herbs," she said, very slowly. "The ones that have taken me a year to grow…" Brian thought that now would be a good time to disappear for a while.

When Wimple had calmed down, she mixed the spell, muttering to herself about stupid dogs and cats, and managed to restore Montgomery to his previous furry self, none the worse for wear. But then she dropped her recipe book into the cauldron and it disintegrated in a puff of smoke.

That was the last straw. Wimple was literally hopping mad. She jumped up and down and stamped her feet, hopping all over the room. Then bump! Her head hit the shelf where she kept all her secret jars and bottles. A big dusty jar marked Frog Mixture teetered on the brink, then fell over, the thick green liquid pouring down onto Wimple's head.

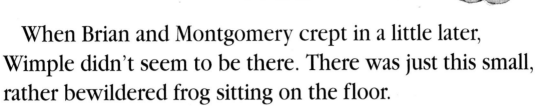

When Brian and Montgomery crept in a little later, Wimple didn't seem to be there. There was just this small, rather bewildered frog sitting on the floor.

Brian looked up at the shelf where all the bottles were higgledy piggledy and saw the upturned jar. He looked at Montgomery and Montgomery looked at him. Then they both looked at the frog.

They ran over to where Wimple's recipe book was kept, but there was no sign of it anywhere! Brian and Montgomery would just have to try and remember the right spell between them. Montgomery rushed out into the garden and nibbled off some squashed herbs. Brian took down the jar marked Pickled Slugs and another that said All Purpose Slime — Top Quality. They mixed all the ingredients together in a spare pot and stirred it with their paws. The frog looked on and blinked silently. Together, the cat and dog sat and

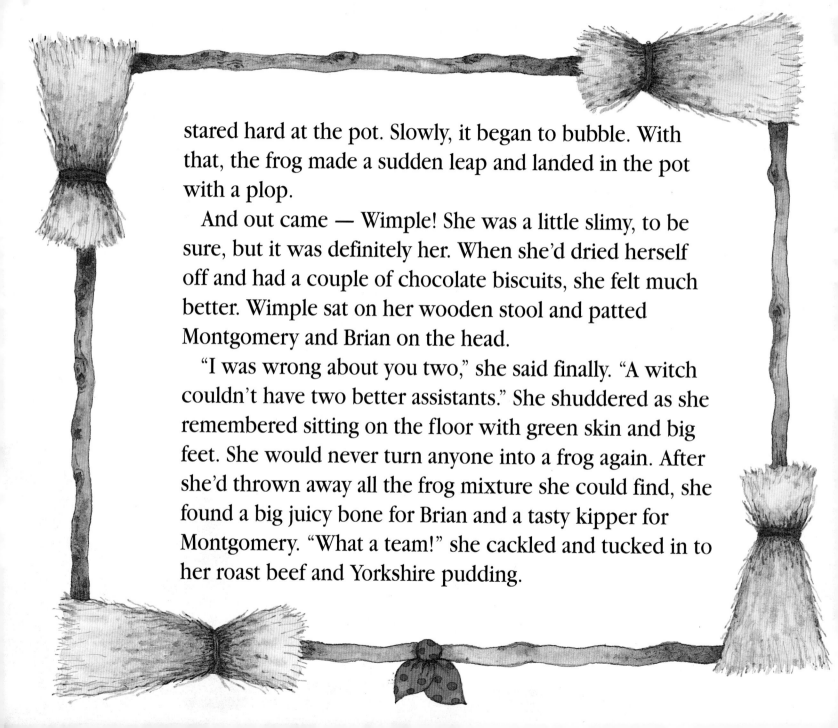

stared hard at the pot. Slowly, it began to bubble. With that, the frog made a sudden leap and landed in the pot with a plop.

And out came — Wimple! She was a little slimy, to be sure, but it was definitely her. When she'd dried herself off and had a couple of chocolate biscuits, she felt much better. Wimple sat on her wooden stool and patted Montgomery and Brian on the head.

"I was wrong about you two," she said finally. "A witch couldn't have two better assistants." She shuddered as she remembered sitting on the floor with green skin and big feet. She would never turn anyone into a frog again. After she'd thrown away all the frog mixture she could find, she found a big juicy bone for Brian and a tasty kipper for Montgomery. "What a team!" she cackled and tucked in to her roast beef and Yorkshire pudding.

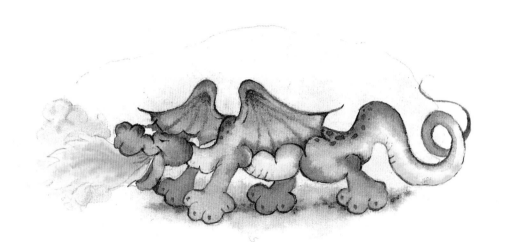